Bein' Good

Jada Jones

EDUCATIONAL PUBLISHING

Bein' Good

Blind Trust

Fitting In

Holding Back

Keepin' Her Man

EDUCATIONAL PUBLISHING
www.sdlback.com

Copyright ©2012 by Saddleback Educational Publishing

ISBN-13: 978-1-61651-773-1
ISBN-10: 1-61651-773-5
eBook: 978-1-61247-335-2

Printed in Guangzhou, China
0112/CA21200064

16 15 14 13 12   1 2 3 4 5

—
[chapter]

1

Kiki sat in Mr. Crandall's office. "Miss Shemeka Butler. Will you please look up and pay attention? I'm attempting to educate you."

Kiki sighed and moved her braids out of her face. Mr. Crandall was the worst. He was always telling students what to do.

"It's Kiki, Mr. Crandall," she whispered. Not like Mr. Crandall was listening. Not a lot of people did when Kiki talked.

"Miss Butler, do you know why you're here?"

"'Cause you got nothing better to do?" she muttered.

—

Kiki covered her mouth. Did she just say that? It sounded like something her twin sister, Sherise, would say! Sherise was always talking back to teachers. Kiki was the good student. The quiet one. Usually, anyway.

Mr. Crandall's blue eyes glared at her over his glasses. "No, Miss Butler. You're a very intelligent girl. You should be able to understand I'm trying to help you."

Kiki frowned. That's exactly what he said when he forced her to join an after-school club. It was lucky that she really liked yearbook club.

"You need to attend class, Miss Butler. It is no excuse that you are doing well. Truancy is not tolerated at this school."

Kiki exclaimed, "I only missed a few days, Mr. Crandall! I was sick. I've already made up the homework."

Mr. Crandall rolled his eyes. Kiki could practically see his hair getting whiter.

Kiki couldn't believe it. Even when she told the truth Mr. Crandall didn't believe her. He never believed any of the kids.

"Then can you explain to me why you let Jackson Beauford copy your work again? Last time you got a warning. I told you if you were caught a second time there would be consequences."

Kiki sighed. It wasn't her fault Jackson sat behind her in study hall. Jackson was nice to her. He noticed her. Sort of.

There was only one other guy who'd ever smiled at Kiki like that, and she'd only seen him a couple of times on the basketball court.

It wasn't like she had a lot of options. Was it the worst thing in the world that Jackson looked over her shoulder sometimes?

"This just isn't the behavior I'm used to from a girl like you, Miss Butler. Until two months ago you were an exemplary student. Then you let that boy copy your homework. Now you're skipping class. What's next?"

Kiki looked at her shoes. What was she supposed to say? That she got so sad sometimes she felt sick? That she really wanted a boyfriend, but didn't know how to get guys to like her?

"Letting boys copy your school work only leads to trouble, Miss Butler. You will not make friends that way. You may think he's cute now, but he'll leave you in the dirt once he gets what he wants."

Kiki couldn't believe it. Yeah, she thought Jackson was cute. Yeah, she wanted him to ask her out, but it wasn't like Kiki really wanted Jackson. She just wanted a guy to pay attention to her. Like every guy in the room paid attention to her sister whenever she showed up. Mr. Crandall had no clue what he was talking about.

"Miss Butler. You seem to be having problems because you don't fit in. Look at your sister. She may not have the best academic record, but she is quite popular. She acts like a young lady should."

Kiki's mouth dropped open. Mr. Crandall was telling her to be more like her sister? Her sister, who didn't like school and rarely studied? Her sister who was in here once a week?

"You might have more friends if you didn't dress like a gangbanger and shoot baskets by yourself so often."

Kiki looked down at her loose shirt and low-riding shorts. So what if she didn't dress in pink like Sherise? So what if she would rather shoot hoops than discuss makeup and hairstyles? She didn't make friends as easily as Sherise did, especially boyfriends.

"Your behavior in here is only the first example. A young lady like your sister would have behaved more appropriately. Try acting more like her, Miss Butler. Then you might have more friends and a real boyfriend. Not one you bribe."

Kiki felt she might cry. What if Mr. Crandall was right? Would Kiki really be more popular if she was more like her sister? Did she really bribe people to be her friends?

"Furthermore ..." Mr. Crandall kept talking.

Kiki stopped listening. Mr. Crandall didn't know anything about her before. He didn't know anything now. Besides, Sherise always came back crying from her talks with Mr. Crandall. He was always trying to make people change.

"... And I think you just need more structure. I'm going to assign you to tutor one of your science classmates." Mr. Crandall looked through the papers on his desk.

"That's so unfair! I already have enough homework, Mr. Crandall," Kiki told him.

"Well obviously you have time to contemplate skipping school. So you'll have enough time to tutor someone else. Be quiet now. I have to find that student I was looking for."

Kiki fumed. Tutoring? On top of yearbook club? And all because she was sick! Mr. Crandall definitely had it out for her.

Kiki knew it was because Mr. Crandall and the science teacher, Mr. Colbe, were friends. Mr. Colbe was an awful teacher. Kids goofed off in his class. Kiki was the only one who was passing. Mr. Crandall was just protecting him.

"Ah ha! Here it is. Tia Ramirez. She's new. Mexican or something. Do you know her?"

Kiki knew Tia. Tia was in yearbook club because she wanted to be. She was also always nice to Kiki. Kiki didn't want to tutor anybody, though. How was she going to keep being the best student if she had to help someone else?

Kiki looked at the clock. Yearbook club started five minutes ago! She didn't want to be too late. It was the only hour of the day she could stand. Ms. Okoro, yearbook club adviser, said she had a special announcement. Mr. Crandall probably didn't even care that Kiki was late. He just kept talking and talking.

Kiki began tapping her toes. Then her fingers. Finally she just jumped into his speech.

"Mr. Crandall, I was supposed to be at YC ten minutes ago. Can I go?"

"YC? What's that? I don't keep up on all your slang terms."

"YC? Mr. Crandall, it's yearbook club. You assigned it to me, remember?" Mr. Crandall was so clueless.

"What? Well, I suppose you can go," Mr. Crandall said. Kiki grabbed her bag.

"Remember, you have to meet with Tia at least twice a week. I don't want to see you back here."

"Bye, Mr. Crandall," she said, walking out the door. She was glad to finally be out of there!

"Oh, and Kiki?" Mr. Crandall had stuck his head in the hallway. "Don't forget to act more like a girl. You might just get what you want."

Kiki blushed. She was so embarrassed. She jogged away, pretending she hadn't heard him. She hoped nobody else had seen or heard him.

She got to the YC room. She sighed with relief. It didn't look like they'd started yet. Everybody was still sitting around talking.

Of course most of the group was hanging around Sherise. Sherise was wearing a pink low-cut top and her hair looked perfect with a cute matching headband. Kiki could never dress like that.

Sherise was talking to a bunch of the girls. Probably about the upcoming dance and how many boys had already asked her. Kiki could see Marnyke, Nishell, and Tia all crowding around Sherise. Kiki went to sit in the back, but Sherise waved her over.

"Girl, where you been at? You look like you been run over or somethin'."

Kiki squeezed her way into the circle. "I just got preached at by Crandall."

"Lord. Nobody likes that!" Nishell jumped in.

"What were you in for? You never go down there. You're the good one." Marnyke giggled when both sisters glared at her.

Kiki grinned. "Yeah, well, Mr. Crandall seems to think Sherise here is the bomb. He told me I should be more like her, and I got in trouble because I was sick. He said I have to do tutoring."

Kiki turned to look at Tia. "Can you believe him, Tia—" Tia caught Kiki's eye and shook her head. Kiki shut her mouth. It seemed like Tia didn't want anyone to know.

Sherise jumped in. "No way! He's always telling me to be more like you, Kiki," Sherise exclaimed. "Mr. Crandall is so two-faced." All the other girls nodded.

"Don't let him get you down," Marnyke said. "Besides, you got to get pumped up for the dance on Saturday."

Sherise rolled her eyes. "Not all of us have dates with the finest guy on the block, Mar."

Marnyke looked at Sherise. "You were just tellin' us how many guys you turned down. Besides, I don't know if I want to go with Darnell this time."

"Come on, girl. He's got it so bad for you. No way he'll let you go alone," Nishell told Marnyke.

Suddenly, a loud whistle came from behind them. Ms. Okoro was usually pretty quiet, but her whistles could be heard all the way down the hall. They all turned to face her.

"Okay. Now that I have your attention, I have two things to share with you all before we start the meeting. The first is a proverb from my country, Nigeria. I want you to listen and tell me what you think it means. 'It is from the small seed that the giant Iroko tree has its beginning.'"

Everyone thought for a minute.

"Is it, like, something to do with gardening, Ms. O? You know that's for, like, old people, right?" Jackson joked from the corner.

"Nooo." Ms. Okoro looked around the room. "Anyone else have an idea?"

"We all start out small and then grow up to be big?" Nishell offered.

"Sort of. Why don't you guys think about it for a bit? My other announcement is a bit more exciting. It has to do with the dance Saturday night."

Everybody stopped talking to listen. What could YC have to do with a school dance?

[chapter]

2

A girl named Misha called from the back of the room, "Go ahead and tell us, Ms. O. Don't leave us hangin'!"

"Well, the yearbook club and the dance team are going to co-sponsor the dance!"

Jackson and Darnell hollered. Someone whistled. A few girls even squealed. Kiki rolled her eyes. She couldn't see why everyone was so excited about it.

Sherise leaned over. "Kiki, this means *we* get to be in charge of the dance. The yearbook club will get a lot of the money too. And even better, everybody knows the clubs that sponsor the dances can get away with *anything*."

Kiki shrugged. She still didn't see the big deal.

"The dance team already chose the theme," Ms. Okoro continued.

Several people groaned.

"But I think you guys will like it! The theme is West Africa. As many of you know, Nigeria is in West Africa. I know a number of you have West African backgrounds as well. There is something for us all to learn about."

"What's some country I don't know nothin' about got to teach me? I ain't even from the west side of town," Jackson joked from the back.

"Well, Jackson, you could always try to figure out what the proverb I said before means. It's a popular Igbo saying where I'm from. It's said only a fool misses out on great wisdom by dismissing a proverb."

"Nah, man. That sounds like too much work," Jackson said.

"So you'd rather stay a fool, then?" Darnell whooped.

"Boys," Ms. Okoro said warningly. "Jackson, if the words aren't something you're interested in, then perhaps you'd be more attracted to the music."

She hit the play button on an old CD player on her desk. Heavy drumbeats filled the classroom. Any excuse not to do actual work was good. Plus, the music was bumpin'.

Ms. Okoro taught them some dance moves. Almost everyone got up to learn. Soon they were all dancing around the room.

Only Kiki and Tia watched from the sidelines. They smiled at each other. Kiki knew she was a terrible dancer.

She liked the music but didn't want to embarrass herself. She knew she wasn't going to this stupid dance. Or any of the other ones this year.

Out of the corner of her eye Kiki saw Sherise dancing really close to Darnell. Marnyke looked angry. Darnell was practically Marnyke's boyfriend. It didn't look like it now, though.

When Ms. Okoro finally turned off the music, everyone complained.

"No worries, guys. I'm sure you'll hear a lot of it at the dance. I wanted to make one last announcement before I let you all out early. Because we're sponsoring the dance, we need to provide volunteers to help set up."

Everybody groaned. Marnyke leaned over to Kiki. "Oh man! This means I won't have time to get ready!"

"Now, not all of you have to sign up." There were many sighs of relief. "But," she continued, "the people who volunteer get their names entered in a drawing. The winner gets two free tickets to the dance *and* gets to use the school camera to take photos for the yearbook."

"Wait. Wait a second. Does that mean they'll also be in charge of the yearbook section about the dance?" Sherise asked. Besides being super popular and liked by everyone, Sherise was also yearbook club president.

"Yes, it does," Ms. Okoro said.

Everybody looked around excitedly. The dance section was one of the most popular sections of the yearbook. To be in charge of it would totally rock!

"Whose gonna to say no to that?" Marnyke whispered.

"Yeah! Free tickets would mean more money for my dress!" Nishell said.

"Or more money for my food," Jackson laughed.

"Now, who wants to volunteer?" Ms. Okoro asked.

Nearly every hand in the room shot up. Kiki kept hers down. She wasn't even going to this dance.

"Aren't you going?" Marnyke asked Kiki.

"Oh, she's going," Sherise answered. She reached over to grab Kiki's arm.

"I don't even like dancing," Kiki said. She pulled her arm away.

"Aw, come on, girl." Marnyke nudged Kiki. "You gotta go! Besides, if you really don't wanna go, you can give me those tickets if you win."

"Fine. Fine," Kiki grumbled. She raised her hand. It felt good that somebody wanted her to go. Maybe if she won, she could get up the courage to ask the guy from the basketball court. Or Jackson.

"It's great that ya'll want to help." Ms. Okoro clapped her hands. She was so happy. Kiki was glad she agreed to help. Ms. Okoro was her favorite teacher. "The drawing will be tomorrow. That's it for today. See you tomorrow!"

Nobody needed to be told twice. Almost everyone ran out of the room. Kiki took her time, though. She wanted to talk to Tia. Tia always waited after to talk to Ms. Okoro. Tia was one of the few who really cared about YC.

Kiki waited out in the hall. When Tia came out, Kiki shyly walked up to her.

"Hey, Tia."

"*Hola*, Kiki. What's up?" Tia seemed excited to talk to Kiki. She must have forgotten about the tutoring.

"Well ... Mr. Crandall ..." Kiki stuttered. She felt bad.

"Pfft! I hate Mr. Crandall," Tia said.

"Me too!" Kiki agreed. She thought of what he said before. Was she not enough of a girl?

"You know, I'm really good at science. I just don't recognize all of the English words in the book. The science teacher *es un idiota*, and now I need tutoring," Tia sighed.

"Look," Kiki offered. "We could do our science homework together. Then, if you want, I can just help you with the words you don't know. We could check our answers together."

Tia thought about it. "Okay. It'll probably go faster without a dictionary, right?"

"Right. Besides, I know you're smarter than half the class already. Mr. Crandall *es un idiota grande.*"

"*Sí*," Tia laughed. "Let's head to the library. I have time before I have to go to work."

"All right." Kiki didn't have to be anywhere. Doing homework in the library was quieter than listening to her sister blast music at home anyway.

"I'm working extra hours at my family's bakery so I can have the night of the dance off," Tia told her.

Kiki shrugged. She wasn't sure what to say. She thought Tia was like her. That she didn't like to dance, and didn't have a lot of friends. But she seemed excited about going. "I guess Tia is like every other girl at school after all," Kiki thought.

"I saw Marnyke and Sherise make you volunteer for the dance. Don't you want to go?" Tia asked.

"I guess," Kiki answered. She thought for a moment about how fun it would be to go with Jackson. How all the other girls would stare and want to be her. She shook her head. No way that would happen. Kiki knew when it came to dancing, she had two left feet. Everyone would laugh at her. Then she'd have to spend the week in bed dying from embarrassment.

"You know, you don't have to go with a boy," Tia offered. "You don't even have to dance."

"Uh-huh," Kiki said. Her sister *never* went to a dance without a date.

"I don't have a date either, you know. We could go together if we don't get guys!" Tia suggested.

Kiki thought about it. "Yeah. That could be fun ... but don't make me dance, though."

Tia laughed as they walked into the library. "I won't. I promise."

They sat down and took out their books to study. Kiki was really starting to feel like she fit in for once. She had a new friend. She wouldn't feel awkward at the dance. She felt good.

The doors of the library swung open and both girls looked up. It was Marnyke. It looked like she'd been crying. She marched right up to Kiki.

"Can I talk to you?" she asked. "Alone? Sherise and I had a fight," she added looking at Tia.

Kiki could tell Marnyke was very upset. But that was no excuse to be mean to Tia. Besides, didn't Marnyke have other friends? Where was Darnell? Why did she have to bother Kiki when she was feeling good and having fun for once?

"Can it wait till later? I'm kinda busy with Tia right now ..." Kiki began.

"Fine," Marnyke snapped. "Forget it. It's not like you care anyway." She stormed off.

Kiki was shocked. She and Tia looked at each other. Tia shrugged.

Kiki decided she better go after Marnyke. "Wait a sec," she said to Tia. "I'll be right back."

Sprinting out the doors of the library, Kiki started looking for Marnyke. Kiki ran to her locker, but Marnyke wasn't there. She wasn't outside, either. Kiki was worried, but eventually she went back to the library.

When Kiki walked in, she saw Tia was upset now too.

"How'd it go?" Tia asked her.

"I couldn't find her," Kiki answered. She could tell Tia didn't believe her. Tia probably thought she was hiding something. Kiki knew what that felt like, but she couldn't make Tia believe her.

Tia quickly packed up her bags, telling Kiki she that she had to work and they would have to study later.

After Tia left, Kiki was mad at herself. She didn't say the right thing to Tia or Marnyke. She never knew what to do or say when she was around people. Kiki felt really alone.

—
[chapter]
3

Sherise and Kiki walked to school the next morning. Kiki was dragging from yesterday. Sherise couldn't stop talking.

"And I was all, Tara, girl, you know, you can't say that about Misha," Sherise chatted away.

Kiki was barely listening. She still felt bad about what happened with Marnyke. She waited for Sherise to say something about it. It was too much to hold back longer.

"But Tara was all—"

"Sherise," Kiki interrupted.

—

Sherise turned to look at her. "What is it, Kiki?"

"I wasn't gonna say anything but ... Marnyke was real upset yesterday. You know anything 'bout it?"

"Oh, man." Sherise looked down. "We had a fight yesterday. Marnyke was telling me about her mom, you know?"

"Oh, yeah," Kiki said. "Her mom went somewhere right?"

Sherise made a face. "Yeah, she went to jail. Mar is having a hard time with it. I was tryin' to be supportive. I really was."

"What happened?" Kiki asked.

"Well, she told me I didn't understand. I was all uh-huh, whatever. Remember cousin Jimmy? He went to jail for stealin'."

Kiki rolled her eyes. Sometimes Sherise was so out of touch.

"Anyway," Sherise continued, "then Marnyke was all, 'What was up with you and Darnell at YC?' And I said we were just havin' some fun. Like, whatever, right? It's not like Marnyke owns the boy."

"Oh, Sherise." Kiki could see why Marnyke was upset now. "What are you gonna do?"

Sherise shrugged. "I mean, I feel bad and all, but I dunno ..."

Kiki felt like she was going to cry. It had seemed like Marnyke was starting to like her. Was she going to lose a friend because Sherise didn't know when to keep her mouth shut?

"Look." Sherise stopped walking. "I can fix this. Let me think."

Kiki kept walking. She was mad at Sherise for making Marnyke angry. She wasn't going to be late too!

Sherise ran up a block later. "I got it, girl! You can't be mad at me."

"Uh huh? You think so?" Kiki eyed Sherise. She was jumping up and down.

"Yeah! We'll have a par-tay! At our house. Girls' night before the dance. What do ya think? Come on! It'll be fun! I'll invite everyone! Please?" Sherise hung on her arm.

"Okay." Kiki gave a small smile. At least nobody would say no to Sherise, right?

The whole day Kiki thought about Sherise and the party. Kiki had never had a best friend. Only Sherise, and Sherise was everybody's best friend.

At YC, Kiki watched Sherise invite all the girls. Nishell, Marnyke, even Tia, and Tia barely even talked to Sherise! Even girls who hardly knew Sherise said yes.

Sherise flashed a thumbs up. Everybody was coming! Then she went and sat next to the boys. Kiki watched as Sherise tossed her hair. She was flirting with Jackson and Darnell! It was like the fight never happened!

Kiki looked at her desk. She felt a black mood come over her like a storm. It wasn't that she was jealous of Sherise. She was proud of her sister, but she didn't want to *be* her. Kiki just wished she could make friends easily too. Kiki was always the one against the wall. Sherise was always dancing with all the boys.

Sherise laughed at something Jackson said. Kiki sighed. She started doodling hearts in her notebook, just for something to do. She couldn't watch anymore. She wished Jackson would talk to her. Or that anyone would talk to her. "Maybe Mr. Crandall is right," Kiki thought. "Maybe I don't dress or act enough like a girl."

But Kiki never knew what to do. If a boy looked at her, her heart pounded. Her throat got dry. She could never think of anything to say. Why would any guy even pay attention to her? Yeah, she was book smart, but only teachers cared about that stuff. She wanted to be street smart.

"*Hola*, Kiki? Anybody home?" A hand waved in front of her face.

Kiki looked up. Tia was there, sliding into a desk next to her.

"Hey, Tia," Kiki said. She wondered if Tia was still mad about yesterday. She just couldn't ask.

"You know, *chica*, your sister? She got some voodoo. She can make anybody like her," Tia said.

"Yeah. Tell me something I don't know." Kiki kept doodling.

"*Dios mío*. Hold on. Don't go all dreamy on me. I got something to say," Tia said.

Kiki raised her eyebrows. Tia was talkative today.

"Sherise may got some witch magic. But I want you to know. She ain't the reason I'm coming to girls' night."

"Then why are you coming?" Kiki asked.

"'Cause, *chica*, you cool!" Tia laughed. "I like hangin' with you. I woulda asked you to study with me anyway. I don't need Mr. Crandall telling me anything."

Kiki smiled. Tia wasn't mad! She thought Kiki was cool. Maybe she did have a few friends after all. Kiki's dark mood started to break up.

Ms. Okoro called out. It was time to start the YC meeting.

"All right, I want to try something new today. It'll get our creative juices flowing. I said we'd make some decorations for the dance. So, we're going to make these ..." Ms. Okoro reached into a box under her desk.

When she came back up she was holding a large brown and white mask. It had designs on the sides and a grinning face in the middle.

Marnyke read Kiki's mind and laughed. "It'll just keep your weave in longer, girl."

"Well, then I'd better put some more in." Kiki pretended to rub more glue in her hair with her fingers.

"Nah, girl. Don't go that far. 'Sides, I gotta help you. This is, like, the only project in the whole school I'd ace and you wouldn't," Marnyke said.

Kiki wondered why Marnyke would say something like that. Was she hinting she'd like Kiki's help? Her grades weren't that bad, were they?

"You know ..." Kiki began. She wanted to ask if Marnyke would like to come study with her and Tia later, but she wasn't sure what to say.

"Listen up," Ms. Okoro said. "Now that you're glued to your seats ..." Ms. Okoro paused, "... literally." She smiled. A few students rolled their eyes. "I'm going to draw the name for the tickets."

She reached into a bowl on her desk. Everyone leaned forward. Waiting.

"Ah ha!" She pulled out a slip. "The winner is ... Jackson Beauford!"

"Ooooh!" It was from a group of girls. They wanted to go with Jackson anyway. So did Kiki. Who would he ask? Would he ever ask her?

Jackson leaned back on his chair. "Lad-ies! I be open for business. If you know what I mean. Especially you." He looked at Kiki as she was walking by.

"Boy, don't be getting too full of your-self," she told him. She pushed his chair with her foot. He wobbled for a minute and then fell over. Everyone laughed as Jackson picked himself up off the floor. Kiki thought it served him right.

After YC was over, Tia and Kiki headed to the library. They wanted to get some studying done. Before long, though, everybody else was there too.

Marnyke was talking to Sherise and Darnell. At another table, a bunch of girls from YC were studying math.

"*Chica*? What is this word? Phoso-fir-as-ant?" Tia asked.

Kiki started to explain, "Oh, that just means it—"

She heard a laugh. Across the room, Jackson and Nishell sat at a table. Together.

"Um. It just means ... it ... uh ..." Kiki couldn't think. She could hear Nishell laughing across the room. Kiki wanted to go over there. Why hadn't Jackson asked her to study? It wasn't fair.

"It's the wrong answer again!" Tia muttered to herself.

Kiki refocused. "Which problem you workin' on?"

"I moved on to math," Tia sighed.

"Oh, that one! Wanna know how I figured it out?" Kiki asked. Tia nodded.

"Okay, so I put people in for *A* and *C*. So *A* is Ms. Apis, the janitor. The one with the tattoos. And *C* is Mr. Crandall. So if Mr. Crandall and Ms. Apis ..."

Tia started giggling. "Mr. Crandall would run screaming from Ms. Apis. Have you seen him avoid her in the halls?"

"I know! His face!" Kiki said.

Tia made a scary face to look like Mr. Crandall. She pretended to sneak behind the table.

Kiki started snickering.

Tia had to stop. She was laughing so hard she tipped over her chair.

The librarian came up. "Girls! I'm going to have to ask you to leave. Don't make me call Mr. Crandall."

They left quickly. Tia calmed herself for a minute, but then made another fake horrified face at Kiki.

Kiki couldn't stop laughing until she got home. It had been a good day.

[chapter]

4

Kiki lay on her bed. Across the room, Sherise was blasting some rap and doing her face.

It was Friday. The night before the dance. Girls' night. Kiki was so nervous. It felt like there were butterflies in her stomach. She always got butterflies when Sherise planned things. What if nobody had fun? What if nobody wanted to talk to her? She could hide in her room. Alone. While Sherise went out with everyone. It had happened before.

Sherise had been scheming all day. Kiki tried to ignore her. Just thinking about everyone coming tonight made her hyperventilate.

"So, I was thinking maybe tonight we could ..." Sherise began. Every sentence Sherise had said all day had started like that. So far, Sherise had wanted to sneak out, meet the boys, play games, and practice dance moves.

Kiki couldn't handle it. "I gotta go." She grabbed a basketball.

"Ma, I'm headed to the courts!" Kiki called over her shoulder.

"Make sure you be back before your friends come, ya hear? I don't wanna be entertaining no giggling girls," her mom said from another room.

"Fine, Ma. I'll be back." She closed the door to the apartment.

In no time she was down the stairs and at the courts. The courts were in the ratty park between the two buildings. They were beat-up and cracked. Just like everything else around Northeast Towers.

She watched a guy on one of the far courts practice. He was the one Kiki had seen before. The one she'd told herself she would've asked to the dance if she'd won the free tickets. Him or Jackson.

He was good at basketball. He made all his free throws. He was cute too. He looked up and waved. Kiki blushed. She walked to a far court. Did he just wave at her? For real? Her stomach filled with butterflies again. This time in a good way.

She started practicing her layups and free throws. She was just getting the hang of it when she started to feel she was being watched.

She stopped and looked around. The guy was standing on the other side of the court watching her. He grinned and waved again. Kiki shook her head. She must be outta her mind. No way was he interested. Guys never paid attention to Kiki. Unless they wanted something.

She shot another free throw ... and missed. It bounced across the court. Kiki blushed even more. She tried to act cool as she walked over to get it.

He grabbed the ball before she could get to it.

"Hey. I seen you play here before. You good, girl." He tossed her the ball.

She grabbed it. "Uh ... yeah. Me too," she responded. She made a face. Me too? Did that make any sense? "I ... uh ... meant ... what I meant was, I seen you play 'round here too."

He laughed. "Oh, yeah? Nosy ain't you? Miss Nosy, am I bein' watched or somethin'?"

"No! No. I just ... um." Kiki couldn't think of anything to say. She could barely breathe.

"Hey, girl. I just messin' with you. If anybody's been creepin', it's me. You got some sweet moves. I was hoping we could play some ball."

Kiki opened her mouth. She was going to say something when she noticed someone walking up to them. "Jackson!" she called out. He was always hangin' 'round Northeast Towers because Darnell lived there too.

Jackson smiled at her. "I been looking for ya," he said. Kiki was confused. Jackson? Looking for her? Was he joking?

Jackson looked between Kiki and the guy. "Girl, you know my cos Sean, here? He's got some mad reps on the court."

Kiki shook her head no.

"You gotta get going, man!" Jackson told Sean. "Get ready for tonight."

Sean smiled. "Nah, man. I gotta minute." He turned to Kiki. "If I can't play a game with you now, I gotta ask your name, Miss Nosy. So I can look you up."

Kiki smiled. Was Sean flirting with her?

"Cos, back off! Kiki's one of my girls." Jackson threw an arm around her. Kiki was surprised.

"I ain't nobody's girl, Jackson." She shrugged off Jackson's arm. "Ain't nobody asked me to the dance yet." Jackson glared at her.

Sean laughed. "You know? I don't wanna cause trouble so I'll beat it, but I bet I'll be seein' you there. If not sooner." He winked at Kiki. Then he walked away.

Kiki watched him go. Her sister would say he was so fine. Kiki liked him. He was nice.

Jackson looked really annoyed. If he wasn't gonna say anything she was gonna go back to playin' ball. She started dribbling.

"Hey, Kiki?" Jackson asked.

"What, Jackson?"

Jackson looked at his feet. "I'm real sorry about you gettin' caught and all. At school."

Kiki blinked. Jackson? Apologizing? He'd never done that before.

"It's cool," she told him. He smiled. Kiki melted. She could never stay mad at him.

"So. You really don't got a date yet? You still goin'?" Jackson asked.

Kiki felt her face heat up. Was he going to ask her?

"Nah. I don't got a date. My sister will bust my ass if I don't go, though," Kiki said. She waited for him to ask.

"Darnell and Marnyke are going together," Jackson said.

"Yeah. That ain't a surprise," Kiki said. "Lots of people have dates. Last I checked, my sis had four or five."

"Yeah, well. I dunno if I'm going." Jackson shifted his feet.

"What? But you got the free tickets!" Kiki exclaimed.

"Yeah. Well I got a lotta books to crack. Might take me awhile. Maybe if I had some help, though ..." Jackson said. He took her ball and started dribbling. Badly.

"Then what?" Kiki crossed her arms. She didn't like where this was going.

"Well, I'd have time to take a date. Especially with those free tickets." He shot and missed. He picked the ball up.

Kiki kept her arms crossed. Jackson wanted her to do his homework. This happened before. She'd gotten caught. Then he'd ignored her. Until now. She really wanted a date. Maybe if he asked nicely? She waited.

Jackson didn't say anything. He just looked at Kiki. His eyes looked so sad.

Kiki couldn't stand it. She didn't want to cave. She forced herself to look away.

"Well, fine then!" He shot the ball at her chest and walked off. Kiki turned the ball over in her hands. What just happened? She didn't know how to feel or act now.

"Hey, Kiki!"

Kiki turned. It was Marnyke. She was early. Girls' night didn't start for another hour.

"Hey, Marnyke," Kiki called.

"What's up with Jackson? I just saw him. He looked real angry." Marnyke set her stuff on a bench and sat down. Kiki thought she looked tired.

Kiki shrugged. She wasn't sure she wanted to say anything about the whole weird thing.

"You lookin' for Sherise?" Kiki asked.

Marnyke sighed. She rubbed her eyes. "Yeah. Kinda, I guess."

"Well, you know where the apartment is. She's probably in there doin' her nails or somethin'," Kiki said.

Marnyke sighed. "I don't know if I can make it. Everything's just so hard. I've had nobldy to talk to."

Kiki knew what that felt like. She wanted to help. Marnyke's cell buzzed. She waited while Marnyke texted someone. Was she supposed to ask Marnyke what was up? She didn't know what to do, as usual.

"Sherise and I are supposed to hang out before girls' night. We haven't met up since the fight. Not for real," Marnyke told her.

"Why not?" Kiki asked.

"I dunno. Too busy I guess. I mean, she apologized. Then we were gonna hang, but Darnell asked me to the dance. Then yesterday he took me to dinner. Plus on Wednesday, Jasmine, Tara, and I were hangin', and Misha called to see how I was doin', 'cause of my mom and all."

Kiki stopped feeling bad for Marnyke. She got Sherise to apologize? And she's got a boyfriend, and all these other friends texting and calling her. How can she say she's got no one to talk to? Kiki felt angry again. She'd jump out of bed every day if she had that many people to talk to.

"Well, Sherise is free now," Kiki said.

She started shooting hoops again. Maybe Marnyke would take the hint.

"I'm just bummed out, I guess. I feel alone kinda. You ever feel that way?" Marnyke asked.

"Sure, all the time," Kiki thought. Marnyke's phone buzzed again. But Marnyke? Alone? Yeah, right.

"You gotta feel like that sometimes. What with being so smart and all," Marnyke said. "I wish there was a way to copy off your brain. Anybody ever try to do that?"

Kiki gritted her teeth. Was Marnyke talking about letting Jackson copy off of her? How could she know? Was she saying she was a teacher's pet and a loser? She must be.

"You know, I'm trying to talk to you here!" Marnyke told her.

Kiki shot another basket. She didn't say anything.

Marnyke stood up. "You know? I always knew there was a reason you don't have no real friends!"

Kiki felt her eyes water. She watched Marnyke storm across the street. So, what was tonight gonna be like?

Kiki heard the giggling as soon as she walked into the apartment.

Sherise came out of the kitchen with two plates of pizza.

"You're late to your own party!" Sherise yelled. "And you're all sweaty." She walked into the dining room.

Kiki rolled her eyes. As if Kiki really had anything to do with the party.

She threw the basketball into her room. Looking down at her clothes, she could tell she wasn't really dressed for a girls' night. Combing through her braids, she changed into jeans and a

T-shirt. Then she practically ran to the dining room.

The girls were sitting around the table. Kiki slid into an empty seat between Misha and Tia.

"Look who's here!" Nishell said.

"Kiki, finally!" Sherise said.

"We started painting without you," Marnyke told her.

Kiki looked at the table. Beside the pizza were painting supplies and more masks. They looked like the ones everyone made in YC.

"There were some extra masks. Ms. Okoro asked us to paint and decorate them," Sherise told her.

Marnyke laughed. "No, she asked *you* to do it, YC prez. We're all just doin' you a favor."

Kiki looked at Marnyke. She sure was happy for someone who said she was all alone.

Sherise giggled. "You got me."

"*Chica*! Glad you're here. I been waiting forever," Tia whispered to Kiki.

Kiki gave her a smile. "Sorry. Got distracted."

She picked up a slice of pizza and inhaled it. She was starving. Then she started to paint a mask.

"Let's play a game!" Nishell suggested.

"Oh! Oh! I got it!" Marnyke said. "Do, Date, or Die."

All the girls squealed.

"Okay. I came up with it, so I get to ask first," Marnyke said. "Sherise, between Devon, Jackson, and … Carlos, who would you do, who would you date, and who would die?"

"Aw, that's no fair, girl!" Sherise smiled. "Carlos already asked me to the dance."

Marnyke smirked. "You gotta answer."

Sherise thought about it. "Okay. I would do Devon 'cause he's so fine. Date

Carlos 'cause he's so sweet. And Jackson would have to die."

Nishell raised her eyebrows. "You wouldn't kill Jackson for real? He's so funny."

"Okay, Nishell. What would you do?" Marnyke asked.

"Well, I'd do Carlos. Date Jackson. And Devon would have to die."

"Fair 'nough," Marnyke said. "Now, Tia." Marnyke smiled. "Do, Date, or Die. Mr. Crandall, Ty, and Carlos."

"Aw, man!" Nishell said. "You gave her an *easy* one. She likes Ty."

Tia smiled. "I guess. I think I'd choose Carlos for the first one. Ty to date. And I'd totally love to lose Mr. Crandall."

Marnyke said, "Who wouldn't?"

Kiki watched Marnyke. She hadn't said anything about their fight at the courts. You'd never know that Marnyke felt lonely. Kiki went back to painting.

How could Marnyke just switch her moods? It seemed like Marnyke's personality could change whenever. She could get anyone talking, even Tia.

"Hey, Kiki? You coming?" Tia asked.

Kiki looked up. Everyone was walking away. They were going to Kiki and Sherise's bedroom to hang.

"Yeah. In a sec," Kiki told her.

Kiki put the last bit of paint on her mask. She wished she could be like Marnyke. She was still upset. She wasn't very good at hiding her emotions.

When she went to her room, she saw all the girls were sprawled around it. Marnyke, Tara, and Sherise sat on Sherise's bed. Nishell leaned against the wall and Misha and Tia were on Kiki's bed.

Kiki sat next to Tia.

"What do we do now?" Kiki asked.

"Let's celebrate! We finished all the masks!" Sherise said.

"Sounds like a plan," Marnyke said. "Let's have some real fun. Anybody up for some 'punch'?"

Kiki could see Tia wince. Kiki knew that Tia didn't like breaking the rules. At least not when she might get caught.

"I don't know if that's a good idea," Tia said. "Sherise and Kiki's parents are here."

"Aw, come on. Don't be a killjoy, Tia," Marnyke said.

Kiki looked at her shoes. She wanted to stick up for Tia, but she didn't want Marnyke to get even madder at her.

Kiki noticed the bag right next to her feet was Marnyke's. It had some shiny things poking out of it. Kiki looked closer. It was a bottle and a flask! She couldn't see the label. It was definitely alcohol, though.

Before she could open her mouth, she heard Sherise stick up for Tia.

"You know what?" Sherise said. "Tia's right. We should save that kinda 'fun' for tomorrow night. It'll be better when everyone is dressed up to the nines."

Tia looked at Sherise. Kiki saw her mouth "thanks."

"Want to play Truth or Dare instead?" Sherise asked.

"Sure!" Tia said. "Truth."

"Do you really like Ty?" Marnyke asked.

Tia's face got red. "A little."

"Ha! You totally do, girl!" Nishell said.

"Okay, Marnyke, your turn," Tia said.

"Truth," Marnyke responded.

"Are you going to the dance with Darnell?"

"The boy asked me. I said if I feel like it." Marnyke patted her hair. "Nishell?"

"Dare," Nishell said.

"Text one of the boys and see what they're up to."

"Oh, hell, yeah! I wanted to go hang with the boys tonight," Sherise said.

Nishell pulled out her phone. "All right, I'll do it, but then I dare the rest of you to do it too. The first person that gets texted back wins."

Kiki didn't want to text anyone. "I'm not textin' anybody," she said. "Do we really wanna go out?"

"Aw, come on, Kiki. You know you want to," Marnyke said.

"If we're goin' out, maybe I do want some punch after all," Kiki said without thinking.

All the girls laughed, even Tia. Kiki frowned. She wasn't joking. Did they all think she was that boring?

"Punch or no, I'm gonna go meet Jackson," Nishell said. "For sure he's gonna ask me to the dance tomorrow. He was all up on me to go and meet him before."

Kiki felt like she was going to cry. Did Jackson really do that? What about the conversation they had before? Was Jackson just using Kiki for homework? He and Nishell had been hanging out a lot lately.

Sherise looked at Kiki. She could see how Kiki felt. "Yo, Nishell. You don't know nothin' yet. Jackson ain't asked nobody yet. So shut your trap before I make ya."

Nishell looked offended. She stood up. "I ain't gotta do nothing, okay? I was just tellin' it how I see it."

Sherise got off the bed. "Well, how you see it is wrong. I was just trying to help stop you lookin' stupid."

Kiki stood up. She didn't want there to be a fight. This sleepover was supposed to be fun.

"Now see here," Nishell said. Then her phone went off. She smiled. "Looks like I'm right after all."

Kiki was tripping out. Jackson was so fine. She hoped that he wasn't just playing her.

What if they actually did sneak out to hang with the boys? Sherise did it all the time. Darnell lived in Northeast Towers too. The boys were always down in the park.

What would Jackson do if she showed up? Kiki's stomach turned over. Would he still be angry? Would he ask her for her homework again? What if he asked Nishell to the dance instead? Kiki would have to watch. Her stomach was really churning.

"Hey, Kiki," Tia said. "Wanna come with me to the kitchen? I need a glass of water." Kiki got up.

As soon as they were in the kitchen Tia turned to her. "*Chica*, you look green."

"Yeah. Thanks for getting me out of there," Kiki said.

"You know, *chica.* I'm really not against drinking or nothing, and you look like you need something to chill," Tia told her.

"Oh, yeah?" Kiki said. "Only if you have one with me."

Tia looked a little worried. "Okay. Just one, though."

Kiki took out one of the bottles her parents hid under the sink behind the extra paper towels. Who were they kidding with their lame hiding place? She poured two shots.

"Ready?" Kiki asked.

"*Uno. Dos. Tres,*" Tia counted.

At three they tipped their heads back. The drinks burned. Kiki made a face. Tia coughed.

"Feel better?" Tia asked.

Kiki did feel calmer. "Yeah. Let's go back in there."

As they went back to Kiki's room, she wondered how the rest of the night would go. Doing shots with Tia? Tia was usually such a good influence. She was the good girl just like Kiki. How much crazier could this night get?

[chapter]
6

Kiki walked into the bedroom. Nishell had gotten a text from Jackson. Kiki had Jackson's number too, but she would never actually text him. Even on a dare. She wished she could, though.

"Jackson says that he, Darnell, and a buncha other boys from the hood are hangin' at the park. Do ya know where that is? Are we goin'?" Nishell asked.

Kiki glared. She knew. She wasn't saying anything, though. Nishell was gettin' on her nerves.

"He means the park between the towers, and hell, yeah, we're goin'. We 'bout to have ourselves a good time," Marnyke said.

"All right," Sherise said, "but I gotta fix my face."

All the girls except Kiki spent the next fifteen minutes putting on makeup. Tia borrowed a low-cut top from Sherise. It was cute. It had rhinestones glued all over it.

Kiki sighed. She wouldn't know where to start with eyeliner and eye shadow. It was enough that she wasn't wearing her basketball clothes. At least she had on her nice jeans and her cutest T-shirt.

Her black mood crept over her again. Kiki sat on her bed and pulled her knees to her chest. She looked at the bottle in Marnyke's backpack. Kiki never felt good enough. Not for anyone. She just wanted to disappear once and for all.

Finally, Sherise and the others were done primping.

"Okay, let's go," Sherise said. "But we best be sneakin' outta here. I don't want the 'rents to know. They'll flip."

She turned up her music a little so their parents would think they were still home. All the girls tiptoed out into the hall. Kiki turned around. She saw Marnyke stuffing the flask in her pocket. Kiki pretended not to see. It was none of her business.

"Do you think they'll hear us?" Tia whispered loudly as they unlocked the front door.

Kiki giggled and shushed her. She was starting to feel good. More free. She could tell Tia felt that way too. "Was it that shot we took?" Kiki wondered.

Once they were out on the street, the girls all started talking and laughing loud. "OMG, Sherise," Marnyke laughed. "I can't *believe* we had to sneak out. It's so ... babyish."

Sherise raised her eyebrows. "I seen you sneak out plenty of times, Mar."

"Not no more," Marnyke told her. "I can do whatever living with my sis. She don't care."

Kiki thought it sounded like Marnyke was bragging, but earlier Marnyke had been so upset about it. Kiki wasn't sure what to think about Marnyke's moods. They always seemed to be changing.

"Oh, man! I wish my parents were that cool!" Tara said. "My momma practically stands in front of the door on Friday and Saturday nights."

Within a few minutes they came up to the park.

"Look!" Nishell pointed at the basketball courts. "There they are."

Five boys were sitting and standing on the park benches. The streetlight flickered. A lot of smoke was around them. Kiki didn't recognize who was who until they got closer. Jackson, Ty, Carlos, and Darnell were all smoking. She still couldn't see the guy in the back very well. He seemed familiar, though.

Kiki wondered what they were smoking. Was it weed? Or just cigarettes? Kiki didn't care. She just didn't want to get in any trouble.

When Darnell saw them, he quickly put out his smoke. He stood up and slunk over. He put an arm around Marnyke. "What's going on, girl?" he asked.

Marnyke waved her arms. "Phew. You sti-ink. Don't be standin' up in my grill smelling like that." She shrugged him off and stepped away.

"Aw, don't be like that, sugar," Darnell said. He followed her. They moved away from the group.

"I'm just sad, okay? You don't understand, Darnell. No one does," Kiki heard Marnyke say.

Kiki was confused. Didn't Marnyke like Darnell? Weren't they going together? Didn't look much like it now.

"Hey, girls," Jackson called out. He pulled out a pack of cigs from his pocket. "Any of you wanna smoke?"

Nishell walked straight over and sat right next to Jackson. "Sure, sugar, but I ain't never smoked one of those before. Wanna show me?"

Kiki snorted. She'd seen Nishell smoke plenty of times. She was always out back of the school puffing away. Jackson didn't seem to mind. He handed her a cig right away. Kiki stopped watching. Didn't look like Jackson even knew or cared if she was there.

"If you girls like somethin' a little stronger, Carlos and I got a joint," Ty said. "We're happy to share. You feel me?"

Kiki couldn't decide. She knew she should say yes. It was cool, but she didn't want to smoke. It smelled bad. Before Kiki could say anything, Misha, Sherise, Tara, and Tia walked over to them. Kiki's mouth dropped. She couldn't believe they were going to smoke weed!

"Sure," Sherise said. She scooted next to Carlos. "Let me have a hit."

Tia stood next to Ty. "Hey," he said. "Come a little closer." He pulled her into his lap. She squealed.

Kiki stormed over to an empty bench. Kiki couldn't believe it. Didn't Sherise remember their granddad died from doing drugs? Obviously not. Tia and the others should know better too. Kiki hadn't realized they were all stoners.

She stared out at the empty block. She could hear giggles coming from behind her. Obviously nobody missed her.

Kiki's mood shifted. She wanted to go back to the group. She wanted to be the one Jackson flirted with. She wasn't makin' any friends on the bench. She couldn't stand up though. She couldn't even think straight. What would she say? Who would she talk to? Besides, she was furious with Sherise.

Marnyke sat down next to Kiki. "Can you believe it?" Marnyke said. "Sherise kissed Darnell on a dare! I am so pissed at her!"

"No way!" Kiki gasped. She turned around to look at the group. Sherise was back cuddling with Carlos. She and Darnell weren't even looking at each other. "Who dared her?"

"I did," Marnyke said.

"What for?" Kiki asked.

Marnyke shrugged. "I don't know. I guess to see if she would. I can't believe she did!"

Marnyke took the flask out her pocket and took a swig. Kiki wanted another drink right now too.

"Hey, can a girl get some juice?" Kiki asked.

Marnyke looked surprised. "For real?"

"Yeah," Kiki said. "Look, I'm sorry 'bout our fight earlier and about Sherise."

"Forget it," Marnyke said. "This stuff makes everything better." She took another drink. Then she handed it to Kiki. "You sure?" she asked.

"Yeah," Kiki said. She was sure. She took the flask. There wasn't much left in it. Marnyke must have been drinking this whole time.

If she had been, something was really wrong. It was too much for Kiki to handle. She took a sip from the flask. She sputtered. Her throat felt on fire. This was stronger than the stuff in her kitchen.

Marnyke laughed. "You done?"

Kiki looked over at the rest of the group. Sherise was taking a puff. Tia snuggled with Ty.

"No," she said. She turned the flask upside down and took a few gulps. Her eyes watered, but she kept going until the flask was empty.

"Whoa, girl," Marnyke said as Kiki handed it back.

Kiki shrugged. Her insides felt hot, and she felt wobbly too.

"Marnyke?" she said. "I have a secret to tell ya, but you can't tell anyone. You swear?"

"I swear," Marnyke said.

"The reason I'm in yearbook club is 'cause I let Jackson cheat off me," Kiki hiccupped. She wasn't feeling so good, but she kept talking. "And I think he's cute, but he'll only go with me if I let him copy my homework. I just want people to like me. If I could only go to the dance with him ..."

Marnyke whistled. "For real, girl? Don't let Jackson treat you like that. I mean if you like him, fine, but don't let him use you. You gotta stand up for yourself. Go for what you want, but trust me, I like you just fine without Jackson."

Marnyke was right. She didn't need Jackson using her. She'd show a side of Kiki nobody had seen. Become a new Kiki. One who got what she wanted. She didn't need Jackson using her.

"You don't need to be getting silly over some boy. You gotta be you. Or else you end up like me. Then you just wanna throw your ass off that old water tower for being so fake all the time. Right now I wish I could end it all. So don't be thinkin' that actin' like other girls is so cool. Be you," Marnyke told her. She got up and walked back to the others.

Kiki shook her head. Had she heard right? Had Marnyke actually said that? Kiki wanted to go ask her. She tried to stand up but her legs felt shaky. She sat back down right away. Her head felt funny too. Kiki decided to stay sitting for a bit.

One of the guys leaned over the back of the bench. Kiki turned to see who it was. It was Sean! The guy from the basketball court.

"Hey, Sean." Kiki smiled.

"Hey, Miss Nosy." Sean smiled back. Kiki felt her stomach turn. He was fine. Kiki wondered if he played with girls' hearts like his cousin. She hoped not.

"Why you sittin' here by yourself?" he asked.

"I just ... don't want to smoke right now is all," Kiki said. She wasn't sure how much Sean had heard.

"You know, I heard Marnyke. She's right. You too cool to be actin' like other girls, and you've got a great jump shot." Sean smiled at her.

"Ah, well, thanks, I guess." Kiki really didn't know what to say.

She looked at Sean. He leaned in close. Then closer. He kissed her! Kiki's head swirled. She couldn't tell if it was the kiss or the alcohol.

Sean stopped. "You okay, Kiki? You smell like the stuff Marnyke drinks."

"Yeah," Kiki said. "I had some. So what?" She wanted another kiss.

"Hey, I dig you an' all, but I don't do stuff with drunk girls. It just ain't right. Maybe another time. Come on. I'll take you back home," Sean said. He leaned over to help her up.

Hoots and hollers started coming from behind them. Sean pulled away from her. Kiki turned around to see everyone in the group looking at them. Jackson was glaring right at her. Kiki didn't care.

"Looks like Kiki's havin' too much fun. We'd best get goin', girls," Sherise said.

"I heard you been having a whole lotta fun too," Kiki said. Sherise dragged her away from Sean.

"Wait!" Sean said. Kiki stumbled. He steadied her. "Can I get your digits? Maybe call you sometime? I really do dig you."

Sherise was still dragging Kiki away.

"Sure!" Kiki said. She yelled her number. Everybody was watching them. Jackson kept glaring.

All the way back to the apartment, the girls giggled and asked Kiki questions. Who was that guy? Had she kissed him before? Was she going to the dance with him? Kiki couldn't answer any of them. The chatter made Kiki's head pound more.

When they snuck into the apartment, Nishell asked Marnyke what was up with Darnell. Now they were all whispering about who would go to the dance with whom. They were too giggly and loud. Kiki's mom yelled for them to knock it off. The girls quieted down a little. They didn't want to get caught.

Kiki landed in her bed. She didn't hear if anything else happened with her mom. Kiki was asleep before her head hit the pillow.

[chapter]

7

B*zzzz! Bzzz! Bzzzz!* Kiki's alarm clock went off.

She moaned and rolled over. Her head hurt. Opening her eyes, she looked around. Sherise was already up. She always got up early. The other girls were just starting to wake up.

"Hey, girls!" Sherise said. "We gotta get movin' or we'll be late for settin' up for the dance! Kiki, remember to pack a dress. We won't have time to come back before the dance."

Kiki groaned but sat up. Her head was still swirling from last night. Had she really kissed a boy? She still couldn't believe it.

Bzzzz! Bzzzz! Bzzzz! Kiki turned to shut off her alarm clock. She realized it wasn't making any noise. It was her phone! She flipped it open. She had a new text message! It said, **"Hey Girl. How u feelin'? Hope you had as good a time as I did last night. Sean."**

Kiki smiled. It was sweet of him to ask. No boy had ever paid this much attention to her. She liked it.

Kiki texted back. **"Feelin' good. Gotta get ready 2 go 2night."**

"Come on, Kiki! Grab your stuff for the dance. We're all almost ready, and you're still lazyin' in bed!" Sherise yelled.

Kiki ignored her. Sean texted back right away. **"See u 2night? Save a dance?"**

Kiki gathered her clothes and necessities for the dance in a daze. She didn't notice that she grabbed a long sweatshirt instead of a dress. She just couldn't stop thinking of Sean.

The girls decided to walk to school to set up for the dance. It was a beautiful day outside. The sun was shining directly into Kiki's eyes. She squinted. She wished she had brought sunglasses. Her head was still aching a little.

"Hey, girl! Have a little too much fun last night?" Marnyke whispered.

"Yeah, a little." Kiki smiled. She was glad Marnyke could keep a secret.

"*Chica!*" Tia grabbed her arm. "Tell me more about this boy! You didn't say much last night."

"Well, he's Jackson's cousin," Kiki started.

Nishell shot her a glare. "Keepin' it in the family?"

Kiki gave Nishell a look. Did Nishell know about Jackson? How could she? Kiki only told Marnyke.

Sherise jumped in. "Come on. We all had a lotta fun last night. Right, girls?"

"Well, we saw you having fun with Carlos, Sherise," Marnyke said.

"Can you believe it?" Sherise said. "He wants me to go to the dance with just him! I was all, 'no way, José. I gots three other dates. You can share.'"

All the girls laughed.

"Kiki," Tia said. "Did I tell you Ty asked me for a dance tonight? I can't wait!"

"No way!" Kiki laughed. "That's so great! Tell me more."

Tia began telling everyone every detail of what she and Ty said and did. Kiki smiled. She finally, finally felt like she was one of the crowd. She had friends! Ones she had fun with. She even told her secret about Jackson to Marnyke. It was so good not to feel left out.

The girls got to the gymnasium where the dance was being held. They met up with all the other volunteers and Ms. Okoro. Sherise, as YC president, was quick to take charge.

Kiki watched her order everyone to split into pairs and pick a job.

Kiki looked at Tia first. Kiki wanted to tell her all about the texts from Sean, but before she could say anything, Nishell grabbed Tia's arm.

"Tia and me are partners," Nishell said. It seemed like she was looking right at Kiki. Kiki wondered what was up with that. She wasn't so mean last night. This morning all she did was make nasty digs at Kiki under her breath.

Tia shrugged in Kiki's direction. "Sorry," she mouthed.

Kiki suddenly felt sick. She couldn't tell if it was the vodka from last night or that she was being left out again. Kiki wondered if Nishell would turn Tia against her too. For one minute she had felt part of the group. Popular even. Now she just felt alone again.

Who was going to be her partner now? It seemed like everyone had someone. Darnell and Marnyke. Jackson and another YC girl. The only person left was her sister.

"It's cool, Kiki," Sherise said. "I'll be your partner."

"As if that makes me feel any better," Kiki thought.

Sherise assigned jobs to each pair of volunteers. There was so much to do. They had to set up the DJ's stage, put out food and drinks, decorate the walls with the masks, and arrange chairs in the hall. Kiki thought they'd never get it all done.

Kiki and Sherise were on streamer duty. They hung the school colors, orange and black, everywhere. It was looking good.

"So did you really kiss Darnell last night?" Kiki asked.

"Kiki, seriously. I kissed him on the cheek pretty much. Marnyke dared me to. Everybody knows it's not even a deal."

Kiki raised her eyebrows. "Maybe you should tell Marnyke that," she said.

"The only reason I did it is 'cause Darnell really wanted to go to the dance with her, and she said would if I did. Marnyke's bein' a drama queen and not makin' much sense," Sherise said. "'Sides, that ain't important. Who's this Sean guy? And what's up with you and Jackson?"

Sherise handed Kiki some streamers to start taping up in the hall. Kiki got on a stool to reach higher.

"Nothin' is up with me an' Jackson. I'm *done* with him. Sean texted me this morning," Kiki told her. It was nice to finally tell someone about the text!

"Girl! Really? Go on, then. I like him," Sherise said.

Kiki laughed. "What? You screenin' my boys now, Sherise?"

"Hell, yeah!" Sherise said. "I gotta protect my baby sista."

"You're only one minute older!" Kiki exclaimed.

"Yeah, well. That still makes me older!" Sherise said. "'Sides, you're terrible at judgin' people. You just wanna be everybody's friend."

"What's so wrong with that?" Kiki smiled. She nudged her sister with her foot.

"Girl, you gotta learn to read people. Jackson is no good," Sherise told her.

"Amen to that." Kiki said. She started taping a streamer really high on the wall. As she was reaching, she felt someone push the stool. It tipped over. She nearly fell on her face.

She looked up and saw Nishell walking away. She must have pushed the stool! "Watch your back," Nishell sneered over her shoulder at Kiki.

Kiki was so confused. What was wrong with Nishell? Kiki turned to Sherise. "Girl, what is up with her?"

"Didn't you hear?" Sherise asked. "Last night Marnyke told us all about your crush on Jackson. She was all, 'Kiki doesn't even know what she wants. She wants to use Jackson to be popular.'"

"That ain't what I said at all!" Kiki said. "I just want people to like me!"

"Hey, girl, you don't see me judgin'," Sherise said. "And I knew Marnyke was over the top. I know you don't swing like that. I tried to say somethin'. But I guess Nishell thinks you're out for her man."

"No way." Kiki couldn't believe Marnyke would say something mean like that. How could she?

"But for real, Kiki. Stay away from Jackson. That boy is bad news. He just tryin' to play you. Get you to do his homework and go with Nishell. Sean is cute and nice. He don't want nothing from you neither," Sherise told her.

Kiki knew Sherise was right but part of her still hurt. She'd liked Jackson forever. She always knew it was for the wrong reasons. He used her. Then he ignored her. Until he needed something again.

Sean actually paid attention. He'd texted her this morning just to see how she was. Nobody had ever done that before.

What felt the worst was Marnyke's betrayal. Kiki had never confided in anyone except Sherise before. Never.

Now Marnyke just slapped her in the face. All for some stupid gossip. Sherise was right. Kiki was not a good judge of people. Marnyke was not her friend.

"Sherise, I got bigger problems right now," Kiki said.

She needed to go find Marnyke. Kiki wasn't going to let her get away with it.

Kiki said, "I'll be right back, Sherise." She couldn't listen to her sister any longer. She had to find Marnyke. Get the real story. This was it. She wasn't going to be the old Kiki anymore. She was going to be the new Kiki. A Kiki who stood up for herself. A Kiki who didn't let people walk all over her, forget her, or use her.

She looked all over the gym. She couldn't see Marnyke anywhere. She and Darnell were supposed to be setting up together. Probably skipping out to smoke.

She walked out of the gym on a mission. Down the hallway she saw

Darnell's back. He and Marnyke were standing close together and talking.

"I jus' think you'd better lay off, okay? Ain't nobody perfect. You can't get so down on yourself," Darnell said.

"Yeah. Whatever, D," Marnyke said. "It's not like you got anything like my problems. My family. My grades. Me."

"Don't dis me, girl," Darnell said. "I know you been hurtin'. I dig you. You don't gotta be perfect."

Kiki didn't have time to listen to Darnell's pep talk. She walked up to them.

"Look, I gotta talk to Marnyke," Kiki said.

Both Darnell and Marnyke looked at her. Marnyke's eyes were dark, sunken in, and so sad. Kiki almost shrank away. That's what the old Kiki would have done. "No, I'm going to be different," Kiki thought.

"I need to talk to her alone. Now," she added.

Darnell shook his head. He looked at Marnyke. "Be in the gym, okay?"

Darnell walked away. Kiki shifted from foot to foot. She was so mad. Once the door slammed behind Darnell, Kiki started talking. She couldn't keep all of her anger in anymore.

"Marnyke!" Kiki yelled. "Sherise says you been tellin' everybody my secret. How could you? Girl, you swore it was a secret. I ain't shared secrets with nobody except you and Sherise. Here you go and stab me in the back! I thought we was friends. Guess you're just a two-face and user like the rest."

Kiki couldn't believe all the things she was saying. It felt good to let her feelings out, but she was being too mean. She was starting not to like the new Kiki so much. Marnyke looked like she was gonna cry.

Marnyke looked her in the eyes. "I guess I thought maybe you understood me an' all that."

Kiki didn't stop her rant. "I like Sean not Jackson. I was just confused is all. Nishell hates me now. She gonna tell everybody how cheap she thinks I am.

"You got everythin', Marnyke. You're popular. You got a guy. You got a ton of friends. Why you gotta ruin everythin' for me?"

"Lay off, okay? I had other things on my mind," Marnyke said.

"That ain't got nothin' to do with nothin'," Kiki said.

"Oh yeah, it does," Marnyke said. "I thought you got me. Sherise don't understand. She ain't never had a hard thing in her life. You understand, though. I know you be down 'cause you feel like you got no friends. I get it. I feel that way too, about my family. I ain't got no daddy. My mom's gone, maybe forever. My sister is always workin'.

Kiki stepped back for a moment. Kiki did feel like she was alone without friends. She thought having friends was everything. But she'd never thought about what life would be like without her mother, stepdad, and Sherise. Before she could say anything, Marnyke kept coming at Kiki.

"My life ain't no cakewalk either. Yeah, I got friends. Darnell and I, we jus' friends right now, you hear? But I'm alone a lot. Like you.

"I thought it would be great, gettin' an apartment with my sister. That we could hang and be friends. But she ain't hardly around. She's workin' so we have a roof over our heads. And you wanna know why I'm in YC? 'Cause I'm failin' every class. That's why. Sometimes it would be better if I just disappeared. Or threw myself off the water tower. Nobody cares anyway."

"But ..." Kiki started. It still didn't explain about Jackson.

"Yeah, I told everybody. I guess I just wanted to feel close to the other girls, you know? Plus, you can't be playin' both Sean and Jackson. I see you yesterday flirting with Jackson. Then later you was kissin' Sean. If you really was nice, you wouldn't be doin' that. I was jus' warning Nishell what you was up to. I wish somebody had warned me about Sherise and Darnell."

Kiki was shocked. Is that really what Marnyke thought? She wanted to explain. Marnyke had it all wrong.

"Look, Marnyke," Kiki said. "You told me to be a new Kiki and go for what I want. I'm tired of living in a black hole. So I took your advice, and now you're on me for it! You can't go 'round judging people for what you tell them to do! That ain't right."

"I'm not listenin' to this crap no more. It ain't going to help me," Marnyke snapped angrily.

Marnyke grabbed her bag. She ran out the door. Kiki was left standing alone in the hallway. She was stunned. She wondered what to do. Maybe the new Kiki was no better than the old Kiki.

She didn't try to follow Marnyke. No point in that. Marnyke had still betrayed Kiki's trust and wasn't sorry about it. Not one bit. "Fine," Kiki thought, "I'm not sorry for taking on Marnyke."

Kiki walked back into the gym. Darnell was standing near the door.

"Where's Mar?" he asked.

"Don't know. Don't care," Kiki said. She kept walking.

She found Sherise on the other side of the gym still hanging streamers. "I'll help some more," Kiki said. She picked up a roll and some tape.

"What happened? What did you say? What ..." Sherise turned around. She saw the look on Kiki's face. She shut up.

While she hung the streamers, Kiki thought about what she was going to say and do. First she had to tell Nishell the truth. Then she could deal with Marnyke.

Sherise and Kiki finished hanging the streamers without saying another word. It was getting late. Most of the volunteers had already gone to get ready for the dance.

Nishell was setting up the punch table. Kiki went over and looked at her straight. It was now or never.

"Just so you know, Jackson and I ain't nothin'. I thought I liked him for a little bit, but I don't now. Got it?"

Nishell's mouth dropped open. She had never seen this side of Kiki.

"I don't know what you heard, but Jackson was using me. I let him. He's nice, yeah, but don't get used like I did. It ain't worth it," Kiki said.

Kiki walked away before Nishell could say anything. It would ruin Kiki's moment. Kiki got as far away as possible from the punch table. She sat on the floor across the hall from the girl's bathroom. She could hear everyone laughing and talking while they were getting ready.

In the bathroom, at least two girls were at every mirror. All of their dresses were sparkly, tight, and some shade of pink, purple, or black. Sherise's was all three.

Sherise looked at herself in the mirror. "I wish I had the dough for a new dress! This is the third time I've worn this to a dance. Carlos is gonna notice and think I'm so lame."

"No he ain't," Misha said. "Guys don't pay attention to that stuff. 'Sides, that dress is kickin'. I'd totally wear it. It's my dress that's old an' boring."

Tia looked over from her mirror. "No way, Misha! I love your dress!"

"We should trade!" Sherise said. "Kiki!" she shouted into the hallway. "Where's your dress?"

Kiki looked in her bag and saw the sweatshirt. She realized she grabbed the wrong thing earlier. "I dunno," she said.

"Girl, do not tell me you did not bring a dress!" Sherise said. "We're all tradin', and I know you have that black one."

"No worries," Nishell walked up. "I brought an extra. Borrow it." Nishell threw a dress at Kiki. Then she walked away. Kiki watched her go. Did this mean she and Nishell had a truce?

"Well, *chica*?" Tia asked. "You gonna put it on or what?"

Kiki changed in a stall. The dress felt really short, and it was very shiny. The shoes Kiki had remembered to bring were strappy and high. When she came out, the girls whistled and hollered.

"Oh. My. God. Kiki, you look so hawt!" Sherise said.

"Yeah. Totally cool," Tia added.

Nishell had come in. She was doing her makeup in the mirror. "Nice," she said.

Kiki smiled. "Thanks for the dress, Nishell," she said.

She did look good. She didn't even want a guy tonight. It was nice to feel cute once in a while. Just for you. It was even better to have friends. After that thought, Kiki felt a pang of fear. Where was Marnyke? They'd fought a while ago. Kiki hoped she was okay.

When everyone was ready, they all left the bathroom together. They walked down the hall toward the gym. "So, have you heard?" Misha asked Tia. "Jackson hasn't asked anyone to the dance."

"Yeah. That's only 'cause I woulda turned him down," Nishell said.

"Sure, girl," Tia said.

"But he's got that free ticket!" Misha said. "And the camera for YC."

"Well, maybe he sold it or somethin'," Nishell said. She sounded upset.

"Hey, I can hear the music!" Kiki said, changing the subject.

"We should head in soon. Sounds like it's time to get down." Misha started dancing toward the ticket table.

The girls all bought their tickets and headed in. The gym looked amazing with all of the decorations. Everyone did a great job to make the place look fun.

Kiki gasped when she saw the room. It was completely different. The lights were down low. All the streamers and masks were kinda spooky and kinda cool too. The DJ was playin' some hot African beats. A lot of kids were really into it.

Kiki looked around. No Marnyke. She started walking through the dancers. Still no Marnyke. Kiki began to worry. It had been two hours since their fight.

"Kiki!" Sherise grabbed her arm. "Oh my God, girl. Have you seen Marnyke? Do you know where she went?"

Darnell was standing behind Sherise. He was still looking through the crowd.

"Not for a while," Kiki said. "What's the deal?"

"When was the last time you saw her?" Sherise asked.

"You're really starting to freak me out, Sherise," Kiki said. She hoped Sherise was overreacting.

"Darnell's been looking for Marnyke ever since you guys finished your talk in the hall. He can't find her anywhere," Sherise said.

"Maybe she's just chillin' somewhere else," Kiki suggested.

"It gets worse, girl," Sherise said. "I wasn't worried either, but then ... Darnell, show her the text."

Darnell held up his phone. The screen flashed. It had a text from Marnyke. "Forget about me. I'm never comin' back."

[chapter]

9

Kiki's stomach dropped. This was all her fault. She should have seen Marnyke was in a black hole and helped her, not yelled at her. It was in her eyes, but Kiki was busy playin' the new Kiki.

"Marnyke and I had a huge fight. It's all my fault she's in a real bad way," Kiki blurted out. "We gotta do somethin'."

"We could tell a teacher. What about Ms. Okoro?" Sherise suggested.

Darnell shook his head. "Can't," he said. "Marnyke was drinkin' all through set-up. Don't want to get her in more trouble."

"What, like she isn't in trouble now?" Sherise asked. She shook her head. "Fine. Let's just look for her."

"We know she's not at the dance," Kiki said. "We gotta search the school for her."

They went through the rest of the first floor. They didn't find anything except a couple of students making out. Marnyke wasn't on the second floor either.

"I don't know if she's in school," Darnell said.

Sherise's phone started buzzing. She pulled it out. The screen flashed Marnyke's name. Sherise looked at the message. She gasped and showed it to Kiki and Darnell. **"Darnell's all yours. I'm gonna jump and end it all. I hate this place."**

"Where is she? How are we gonna help her?" Darnell was frantic.

Sherise snarled, "I don't know, fool! Don't you think I'd be there already?"

"Calm down," Kiki said. "We can figure this out. She's gotta be someplace high if she said somethin' 'bout jumping. What's the tallest thing near here?"

Sherise snapped her fingers. "The old water tower! It's only three blocks."

"She did mention that to me earlier. Something about throwing herself off a tower," Darnell said.

"Yeah, I heard that too," Kiki said. "We got to go now."

Kiki, Sherise, and Darnell all tore out of the high school like they were being chased. The two girls even ran all the way there in their strappy heels.

They were all panting by the time they got there. It was getting dark. Kiki squinted her eyes at the old water tower. It looked like someone was up there. She couldn't be sure.

"Marnyke! Marnyke! You up there?" Darnell started yelling.

"Look who finally showed up. Darnell, the boy." Marnyke's voice was thick. Kiki could tell Marnyke was drunk.

"Marnyke! I'm comin' to get you!" Darnell said. He grabbed onto the rusted ladder of the old water tower. His foot went straight through the first rung. The whole tower shook.

"I don't know what you doin' down there, boy, but don't you come up here! I'll jump. I swear I will," Marnyke slurred.

"Marnyke. Can I come up?" Sherise shouted.

"Oooh, look! Sherise, the girl! Aren't you guys just the greatest pair?" Marnyke said.

"I'm coming up!" Sherise said. She started walking toward the tower.

Something fell from above. "Look out!" Kiki screamed. Darnell stepped out of the way just before a bottle smashed on the ground.

"Ooops!" Marnyke said. She laughed. "Well, I was done anyway."

"We gotta figure out a way to get her to come down herself," Kiki whispered. "If you guys start climbing up, you might shake it enough to make her fall."

"Well, what are we supposed to do?" Sherise asked. "She's not listening to Darnell or me."

"Oooh, look at the flashing lights, you guys!" Marnyke said.

Kiki, Sherise, and Darnell turned around. They heard the sirens coming. The flashing lights came into view.

"Damn," Darnell said. "The cops. They're not gonna help."

"I'll go talk to 'em," Kiki said. "You guys just keep talking to her. Don't let her jump."

The first police car came to a stop. There was a male and a female officer in the car. The male officer got out on the passenger side. Kiki quickly ran up to him.

"You have to stay here," Kiki told him. "My friend. She's up there. She's been drinking, and she's about to jump."

The officer looked her up and down. Kiki could tell he wasn't impressed. She remembered she was wearing a short, shiny, blue dress. She blushed and wished she was wearing her regular clothes.

"Don't worry, little girl." The officer looked like he was going to walk right past her.

"Wait! The water tower is old. If you try to climb it, you'll knock her off," Kiki cried. She tried pulling him back. He shook her off.

"We're trained to handle this stuff," the officer said. He was still walking to the tower.

The driver had gotten out. She called out, "Wait, Johnson." The male officer stopped and turned around. The female officer looked at Kiki. "You think you can get her to come down?" the woman asked Kiki.

"I don't know," Kiki said truthfully, "but I sure as hell have a better shot than you two."

The woman eyed her. "All right. You got ten minutes. That's when backup gets here. After that I can't promise anything."

Kiki sucked in a breath. Ten minutes to save Marnyke's life. Kiki turned and ran to the water tower.

Kiki heard Sherise pleading with Marnyke. "The cops are here, Mar. You just gotta come down." It sounded like Sherise was crying. Kiki felt like she was gonna cry too.

"You know I'll jump 'fore I let anyone near me," Marnyke said.

Kiki ran past Sherise.

"Marnyke!" Kiki yelled. "You still up there?"

"Who's that?" Marnyke said. "Kiki? Yo, girl. You must want me to jump off this thing. You'd never have to see my face again."

"Hold on a minute," Kiki told her. "Just hold on."

"What! You gonna try to climb up here?" Marnyke yelled.

"No. I just wanna talk ..." Kiki frantically tried to think of something to say. Something that Marnyke would listen to.

"It doesn't have to be like this, you know. You know I feel like you do sometimes," Kiki continued.

"It's never that bad for you," Marnyke said.

"Sure it is," Kiki said.

"Yeah, right." Marnyke wasn't listening. Kiki had no time. She had to try something else.

"Hey, remember that proverb Ms. Okoro told us last week?" Kiki asked. She crossed her fingers. This had to work. Kiki had nothing else.

"What, the one about trees and whatever? What's it got to do with me?" Marnyke said.

"'It is from a small seed that the giant Iroko tree has its beginning,'" Kiki recited. "I get it now. It means ... I think it means ... we all start out small and alone, and we grow up to be big an' strong. We gotta go through a lotta stuff to get there. You and me, we just feel like a small seed longer than other people, but someday we'll be the ones making the forest."

Marnyke was silent for a minute. Kiki held her breath

"You think?" Marnyke said wistfully.

"Yeah," Kiki said. "I really do, but you gotta wait. If you never give it a chance, how will you know?"

"I guess I wouldn't," Marnyke said.

"If you come down, we can all give it a shot together. You, me, Sherise, and Darnell," Kiki told her.

Marnyke sighed. She turned around. She started down the ladder. "I should just jump off," she said.

Kiki froze. It hadn't worked. She felt her eyes well up. Would Marnyke jump off now? Or would she wait for the cops to knock her down?

Marnyke continued, "But I'm coming down. I guess I can give the growing thing a shot."

Kiki sighed with relief.

Marnyke climbed down the ladder. But not quickly enough for Darnell. He grabbed her before her feet hit the ground. Sherise and Kiki ran over to them. They all hugged Marnyke at once.

"Does this growing up include feelin' squished?" Marnyke asked.

"I don't know," Kiki said, "but it sure as hell beats feelin' alone."

"Damn straight," Marnyke said.

"Don't you do that again, Mar! Not ever!" Sherise said. "I always got your back, no matter what it seems like."

"Me too," Darnell said.

The cops were walking up. "You kids better back off now. This girl is going to get a ticket and a police visit at home now," the female officer said.

"I'm coming with her," Darnell said. He looked at Marnyke. She smiled a little and nodded. It seemed like they might be friends after all.

"We'll see you tomorrow morning," Sherise said. "We promise." Kiki nodded.

The police, Darnell, and Marnyke started walking toward the car when Marnyke turned around. She came back to Sherise and Kiki.

She gave them both another hug.

"Thanks," she said. "Have a great time at the dance tonight, okay, you two? I want to hear all about it."

"We'll go back. Do it for you, Marnyke," Sherise said.

"I know you will, Sherise. And Kiki?" Marnyke turned. She looked Kiki in the eyes. "You gotta go. Go dance your heart out. Live it up. You might think you're shy. You might feel alone. But, girl, you growin' faster than anybody I know. I mean it. Make it your moment." Marnyke turned and went back to the cop car.

Sherise and Kiki watched them drive off. Kiki wondered if she was really growing. Could she really do what Marnyke said? Make it her moment? It had never felt like it was her moment. She still felt alone. Inside, Kiki was still so much like Marnyke, but maybe the new Kiki had grown a little.

Another cop car showed up pretty soon after the one driving Marnyke and Darnell left. The cops stopped Sherise and Kiki. "You'll have to give us your statements," one of the officers said.

Kiki and Sherise told them what happened. When they finished, the cop said, "We can give you a ride to the dance if you want."

Sherise made a face. Kiki knew what she was thinking. What would everybody say if they showed up at school in a cop car? Their mom would definitely hear about it in no time. No way they wanted to have their mom come and drag their butts home from the dance.

"Thanks, but I think we'll just walk, officer," Kiki said. "It's only three blocks."

The cop shrugged. "Suit yourselves."

Kiki and Sherise walked back to the school slowly. Along the way, they decided not to tell anyone what happened. That was up to Marnyke. They'd tell everyone a story instead.

As they walked up the school steps, Sherise turned to Kiki. "Girl, you know you were awesome, right? I ain't never been more proud of you, Kiki. I know you think I'm brave for talkin' back to Mr. Crandall an' all those teachers, but I could never have done what you did."

Kiki smiled. "I'm just glad I could help Marnyke."

Sherise shook her head. She ruffled Kiki's braids. "Whatever you say, little sister."

The dance was in full swing when they walked in the doors. People were even spilling out into the hallways. Everyone was having a great time.

"Success!" Sherise said, looking around. "The YC will get tons of money for sure!" She gave Kiki a high five.

Kiki and Sherise were instantly swarmed the minute they got back to the dance floor. Everybody wanted to know what happened to Marnyke. They knew the girls were looking for her earlier and had left school.

"Did you find her?" Tia asked.

"Where was she? Did she hurt herself?" Misha wanted to know.

"She must have been drunk," Tara told everyone.

"Or high," someone else joked.

"No," Sherise said. "She wasn't."

"We found her," Kiki said. "She got the flu. Darnell took her home."

"Seriously?" Misha said. "How lame."

"Bet Darnell ends up with the flu too," Devon snickered.

The crowd around the girls quickly broke up once everyone had heard the scoop.

Nishell and Tia stayed with Kiki and Sherise. Tia gave Kiki a hug. "I don't know what happened, but I'm glad you're okay," she said.

Kiki smiled. "Thanks, *chica*. How's your night been goin'?"

"*Estupendo!*" Tia exclaimed. "Ty showed up. He's getting me some punch."

Kiki raised an eyebrow. Everyone knew Ty was always the one who spiked the punch at dances.

Tia laughed. "Some regular punch. I made him promise."

"That's cool," Kiki said. "What 'bout you?" she asked Nishell.

"Are you sure nothing else happened with Marnyke? 'Cause she came down with the flu right quick. I don't wanna be getting sick or nothin," Nishell said.

Tia elbowed Nishell. "Nishell!" she scolded.

"All right! I'll drop it. If I get sick it's on you, girl," Nishell said.

"For real, Nishell. Tell Kiki about Jackson," Tia said.

Kiki looked at Nishell.

"He showed up solo," Nishell sighed. "An' ever since, he's been flirting with every girl whose skirt is up to here." She made a line high on her thigh.

Kiki raised her eyebrows again. It wasn't surprising from Jackson. So why was Nishell annoyed?

"He's been using the YC camera to get girls to dance with him," Tia added.

"Yeah. The fool's been tellin' all of them if they make out with him, they'll get their picture in the yearbook," Nishell huffed.

"Lucky for Nishell, no one's said yes yet," Tia whispered.

Kiki shook her head. Sounded exactly like Jackson's behavior to her. She was ready to move on to someone who didn't act like a fool.

"Have you girls seen how great the decorations turned out? That's what he should be taking pictures of," Kiki said.

"Yeah!" Tia said. "Everybody has been sayin' stuff. Like how it's the best dance ever."

"No, really?" Kiki said.

"Yeah," Nishell said. "Like ten people have asked if they can have a mask. Ms. O is thinking about havin' a mask auction to raise money for YC and dance team. We rock!"

Kiki smiled. That was a great idea. Kiki was starting to think this dance couldn't get any better. She actually felt like she wanted to dance.

Ty walked up. "It's only 'cause the masks are so cool," he said. He handed Tia a glass of punch. Then put an arm around her and smiled.

"Thanks, Ty!" Tia exclaimed. She seemed really happy. They seemed really into each other, and if Ty had been true to his promise, it had nothing to do with alcohol.

Kiki almost wished she had a date, but then she shook her head. She was happy being herself for now.

Kiki's phone buzzed. It was a text from Sean. **"You look good, girl. Still wanna dance?"**

Kiki was confused. Sean wasn't here. Was he? She felt a tap on her shoulder. She turned.

"Sean! How'd you get in? You don't go here!" Kiki said.

Sean smiled. "Nice. First words from the pretty girl and she asks me how I snuck in. You gonna throw me out?"

Kiki blushed. She shook her head. She'd said the wrong thing again. This time she didn't care. She could tell Sean was joking.

"For your information, Miss Nosy, Jackson gave me his extra ticket. Somethin' about not wanting to choose just one girl to go with," Sean told her.

Nishell snorted behind her. "Sounds 'bout right."

"So how about it? Did you save me a minute out on the floor to shake that booty?" Sean asked.

Kiki was about to reply when Jackson walked right up and stood between them. He looked like he was looking for someone else, but then he stopped.

"Oh! Hey, Kiki. Wanna dance?" Jackson asked, ignoring Sean.

Kiki looked between Jackson and Sean. Was this for real? Did Jackson know what was going on?

"Come on," Jackson continued. "No strings attached. No homework. No kissing. I might even put you in the yearbook for free." Jackson winked.

Kiki wavered. Part of her knew all the girls would be jealous, way jealous, if she danced with Jackson. Everyone would want to talk to her. But was that really what she wanted?

Jackson turned. "Hey, Sean, you tryin' to move in on me, man? You promised not to ask one of my girls to dance if I gave you the ticket."

"Hey, man," Sean said. "You weren't doing nothin'. I figured it was cool. 'Sides, Kiki already said she wasn't one of your girls."

"Well, you figured wrong," Jackson said. He pushed Sean in the chest.

Sean looked really angry. He started toward Jackson. Would there be a fight? Kiki didn't want anyone to get hurt. She quickly moved between them.

"Wait!" she said. She waved her arms to separate them. She slapped Jackson's jacket. Something dropped to the ground.

Was it the camera? If they broke the YC camera, they'd all be dead. Kiki bent over and picked the object up. It was an empty flask. One that smelled really strong.

Kiki gave it back to Jackson. "I think you dropped something."

She turned to see Sean shake his head. "Jackson, you're drunk aren't you? Let's jus' drop it." Sean turned. He started walking toward the door.

"So?" Jackson asked. He still thought Kiki was going to dance with him.

Kiki looked at Jackson. "You know what, Jackson? I think you'll just be waitin' this time. Someone's already asked me to dance."

Kiki ran after Sean. She grabbed his arm and dragged him onto the dance floor. He put his arms around her and Kiki smiled.

This was it. For once, it was all the other girls who'd want to be Kiki. It was her moment. Marnyke was right. She was gonna make the most of it.